ISBN: 978-0-578-84829-7

Illustrations, design and layout by Michael Talbot

First Edition

drjoestories.com

Hare never got over the race where he was beaten by Tortoise.
The defeat made him the laughing stock of the Forest.
Days turned into years,
But he could not get over his loss.

Suddenly, he had an idea!
A REMATCH!
This time, he would surely win!
But would Tortoise agree to race?

He asked Owl for advice.
Owl saw new houses going up everywhere
And knew the Forest would someday become
another subdivision.

What if he sold the book and movie rights to
The "Tortoise and Hare Rematch"?
Then they could buy the Forest!

Owl told Hare that he would discuss it with Tortoise
And flew to the riverbank.

"Tortoise," Owl said, "I have something serious to discuss with you.
Hare never got over his loss when you two raced.
He wants a rematch.
Crowds will cause damage and disrupt our life here.
But if my plan works, it might save the Forest."

Said Tortoise, "I can't race without preconditions.
Hare is not going to fall asleep this time."

"What do you suggest?" asked Owl.

Owl went back to Hare, who was upset.
This wasn't going to be a pushover.

CONTRACT

"TORTOISE AND HARE REMATCH"
Book and movie rights

A book and movie deal was made.

Finally, the day arrived!
The World knew about the rematch.
It was being hyped as "The Race of the Century!"
And was to be an extreme race, over both land and water.

THE RACE OF

世紀のレース

¡CARRERA DEL SIGLO!

Rennen des Jahrhunderts!

Corrida do Século!
THE CENTURY!
MBIO ZA KARNE!
La course du siècle!
Гонка века!
מרוץ המאה!
Yüzyılın Yarışı!

Three minutes before the race began,
Hare and Tortoise stepped up to their vehicles.

The crowd gasped as the coverings were pulled away.

Tortoise climbed up into an ATV
While Hare settled into a small tank.

On your mark!
Get set!
GO!!!

Neither of them had much practice driving,
And the crowd had to jump for cover as they went
Swerving up the path.

They were running neck and neck as they neared the water.

Then, Tortoise hit a rock and his vehicle flipped over.

Hare turned to look and hit a tree.

They each had a jet ski waiting on the bank of the river.
Hare had a pair of stilts strapped to the side of his jet ski.
He ran to the water ahead of Tortoise and took off.

Tortoise took off behind him but soon closed the gap.

Up ahead, a huge tree had fallen completely across the river.
Tortoise dove into the water.
Hare quickly unstrapped his stilts,
And began wading down the river.

Tortoise was swimming as fast as he could,
And Hare was making large strides with his stilts.
They crossed the finish line,
Tortoise covered with river slime,
And Hare drenched in sweat.

"It's Hare by a nose!"
Called the judges.

Hare had done it!
Tortoise didn't mind.
In fact, he was happier this way.

Hare basked in the attention he always craved.

Sadly his life was cut short by
a heart attack a few weeks
after the race.

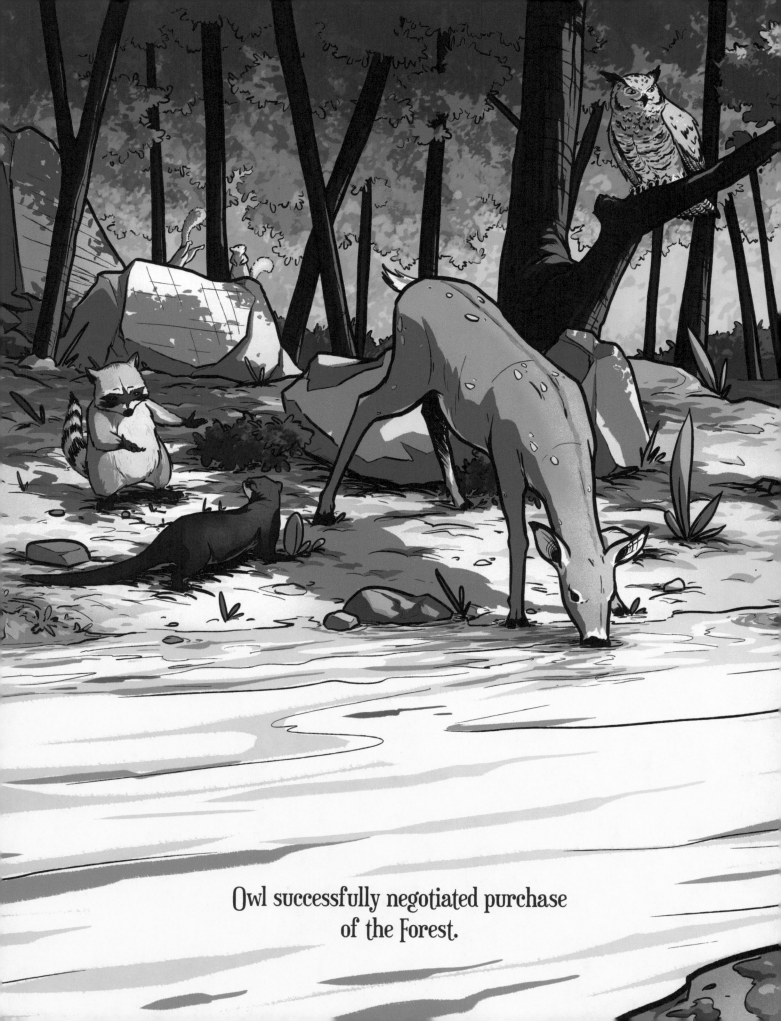

Owl successfully negotiated purchase
of the Forest.

And Tortoise...

... Returned to his quiet life by the riverbank.

CPSIA information can be obtained
at www.ICGtesting.com
Printed in the USA
BVHW061204290421
606128BV00002B/161